GRANDMA WURA'S STORY HUT

Series
I WISH I WISH

Published by Proud African Roots Ltd.
proudafricanroots@gmail.com

Name of Authors: Patrick Edwards
                  Bola Edwards

I WISH I WISH

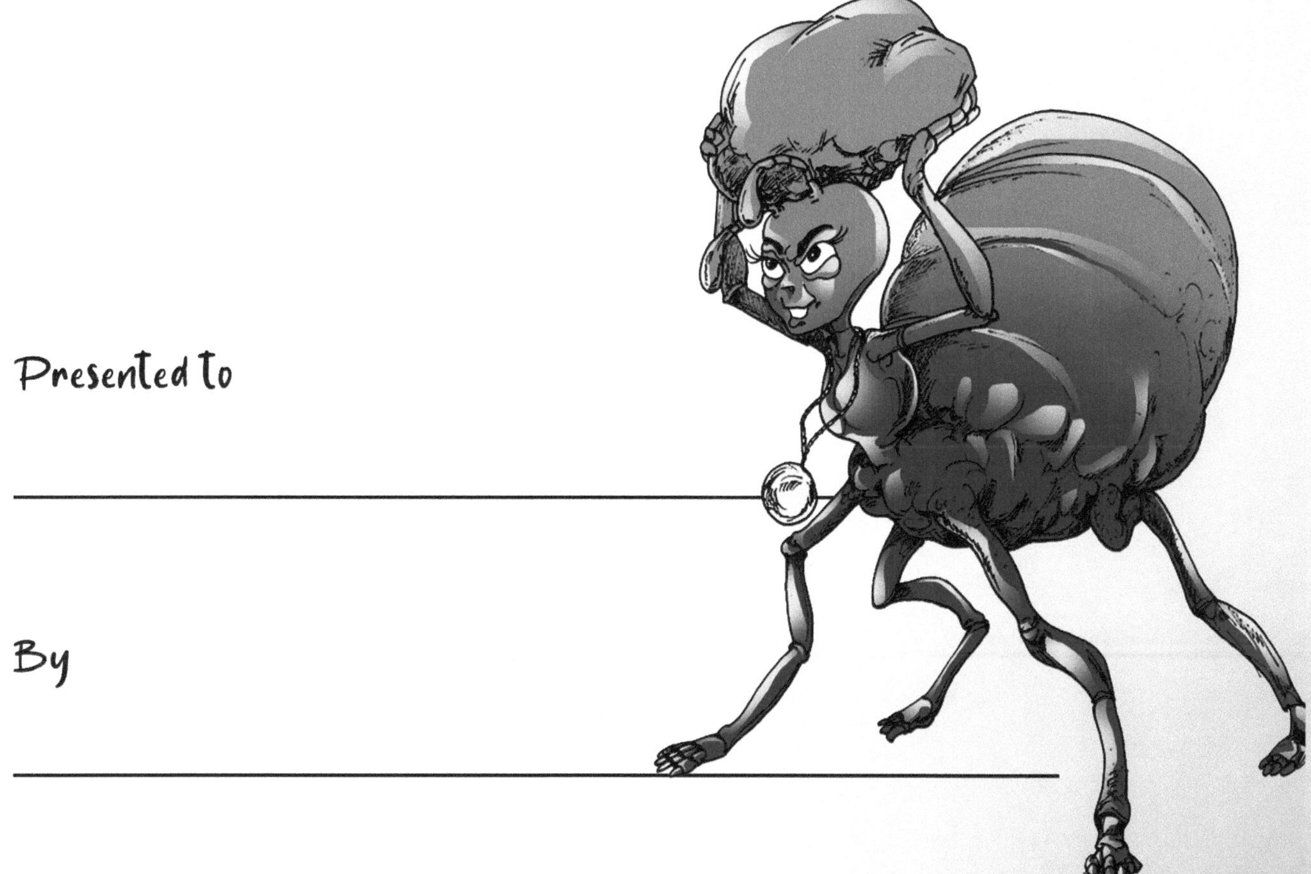

Presented to

____

By

____

Once upon a time, there lived a little girl called Nkechi who always wished that she was an ant, so she could always have enough time to play and do whatever she wanted. She wished so hard to be an ant and not a little girl anymore.

On a sunny Eke market day, Nkechi's mother sent her to the woods to fetch some firewood in preparing dinner.

She grumbled and mumbled all the way wishing over and over again
that she could just turn into an ant so nobody would bother her
with running errands anymore. Unknown to Nkechi, the Wind of
Wishes was out in the woods that day to grant wishes, and as soon
as she made her wish to become an ant, all the trees on the path
where she walked
stood still.

It seemed like the wind didn't blow through them anymore. The birds stopped chirping and singing. Everything around her suddenly went still. Then, there came a mighty rushing wind; it picked her up and spun her in the air. She screamed, and just as suddenly, everything was back to normal; except for poor Nkechi of course. The leaves seemed so much bigger, and the ground, much closer than they were before.

Nkechi, was now breathing very heavily and felt rather
 light-headed. She swayed from the left, then to the right, and
back again as she tried to steady herself... trying to understand
why she felt so unstable. Then, Nkechi looked down at her legs
and exclaimed in horror at what met her gaze. Anxiously, she
staggered very quickly towards a puddle of water on the ground
close by. She was now struggling to fight back the tears that now
stung her eyes as she stared back at her ant reflection in the
puddle of water; when suddenly, she was jolted by a harsh and
very loud voice from behind her.

"Hey, you! …you have been snoozing, haven't you?" Nkechi, spun around very quickly to see who it was that spoke so harshly. She stood, rooted to the ground, too confused to run. In front of her stood an angry-looking ant by the name Opaku, holding a stick-like object, and behind this angry-looking ant, were hundreds of thousands of other ants – busy, working ants.

Opaku, seeing Nkechi was not yielding to his command, hit her on the head with his stick-like object.

"Ewo!" Nkechi screamed, "Bikonu!! Do not hit me with that stick again, it hurts!!! At Nkechi's outburst, Opaku tried to hit her again by moving even closer, "Come on!! Get to work, you, lazy snoozer", he ordered. Nkechi tried to dodge as she gave a long shrill cry, "I-am-not-an-ant! I'm a little human girl."

At Nkechi's cry, every working ant froze in its track and turned to see the little ant that had just lost its mind.

There was a sudden silence, as each ant looked in utter amazement from one to the other and then to Nkechi. Then, almost immediately they all burst into a thunderous roar of laughter.

Nkechi, tried to explain herself as she went from one ant to another ant and then to another saying, "You see, I'm just a little girl who has only lost her way… I really am not an ant… my mother sent me to fetch some firewood in preparing dinner… she would be really worried about me by now", but her words only made the ants laugh harder.

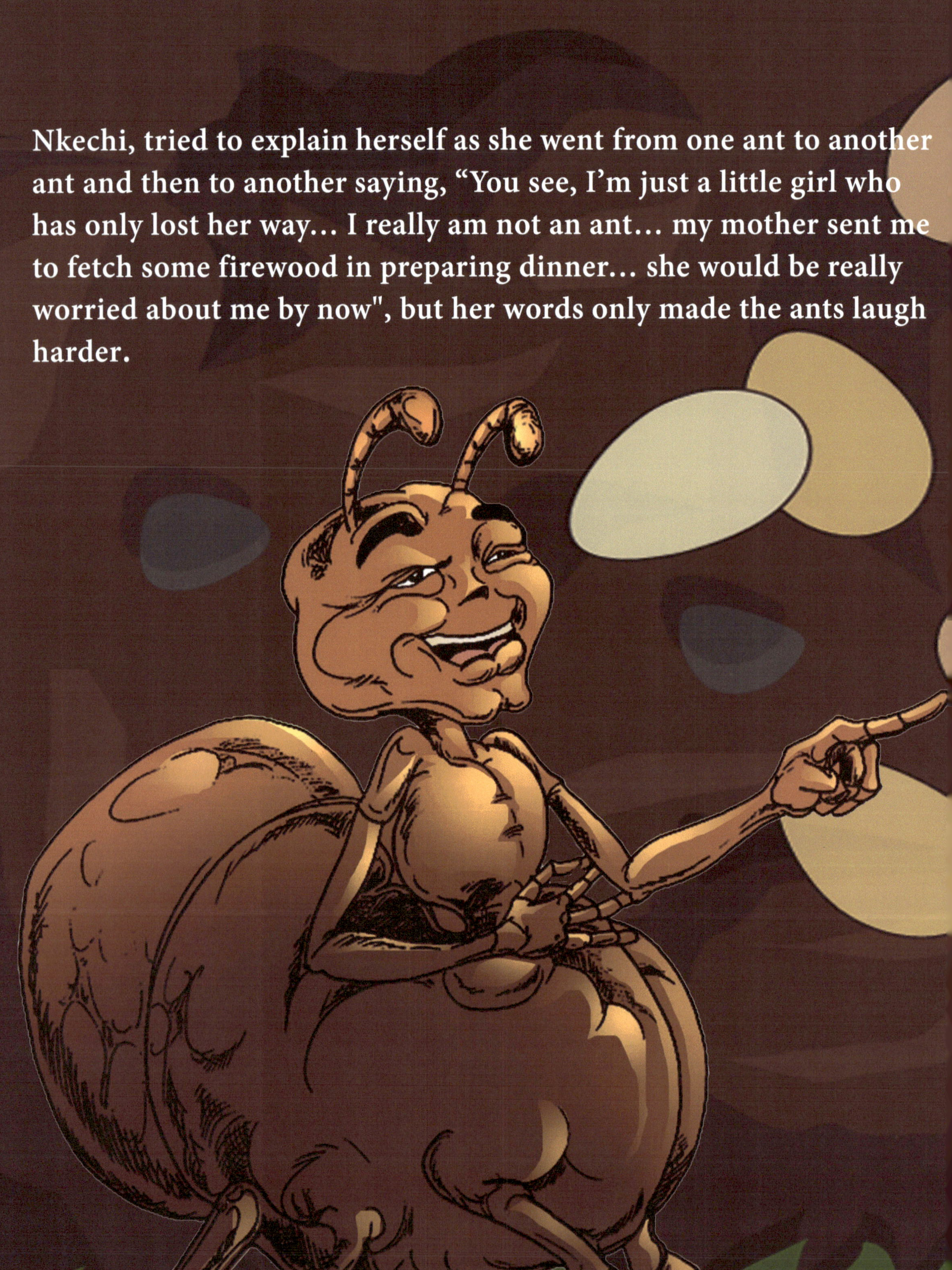

Nkechi, was more confused and frustrated now than ever as she continued to explain; desperately needing and looking for just one ant; that one ant that would believe her story as she pushed her way through the swarm of ants that had now closed in on her. "Excuse me…excuse me please… Oh sorry… I really have to get home now, my mother would be very worried… I really am a little girl…bikonu… excuse me.

A very friendly voice from behind her cut in, "okay, you are a little girl, so what happens now?" It was Ona... Ona was one of the wisest and most caring ant who always looked out for others. She smiled very warmly at Nkechi as she tried to turn her around to face her. Then she said, "I believe you, but where can you go now, looking like this? Your human mother wouldn't even know you were there except she looked very hard. And I bet she won't be expecting to see you as an ant or would she?".

Nkechi shook her head and began to sniff quietly as tears welled up in her eyes."Oh...don't cry little one," Ona said sweetly, as she consoled her. "Come on, let's get back to work before mean Opaku picks on you again." By now, all the other ants had gone back to work, but Nkechi continued to try and convince Ona about the little girl that she really was. Ona only giggled some more, saying, 'I understand how you feel and how exhausted you must be but as ants, we work all day long, as we must feed ourselves and our queen; feed the soldiers, build our ant hills and..." Nkechi cut in, "What?!... you do all that?".

To this, Ona replied giggling, "but of course, you know that, don't you? Or do you play around while the rest of us work?" The tears welled up once again in Nkechi's eyes as she tearfully said, "I didn't know… I…I… told you I am a little…" Ona quickly cut in saying, "Ah! Yes … a little girl, oh yes, I remember that; but why don't you get back to work with me and later we can talk about it… okay?".

All-day Nkechi worked, with barely enough time to rest or play. Nkechi soon discovered that there were no busier creatures on earth than the ants. She was now an ant, but not a happy one. The only true friend she managed to make was Ona. Ona, was the only one who understood her, and she alone believed her story – or so she thought.

Nkechi, discovered that being a little girl-ant was not fun at all and most times as she went about her work, she cried for her mother and her home. She was sorry she had wished to be an ant and hadn't appreciated the girl she was with all she had. Being a little girl-ant had really shown her that her life as a human girl was much better even with all the chores or challenges that came with it.

 Now sobbing very softly and muttering to herself, "I wish I could just go home once again... just to see my mother, my brother, and father; and tell them how much I appreciate them, nothing else. Oh! How I wish I was a little human girl again".

Then, she heard a soft and gentle voice from behind her say; "one thing I have come to know and appreciate is never to wish to be something else and just be the best of me". Nkechi turned, only to find herself standing face to face with the ant queen who was now smiling softly down at her. "I once used to wish I was something else too and not an ant", she said. "However, I have since learned that situations do not define us but how we handle them is what matters. And so, I decided to be the best ant queen that I can be. So little one, never worry about being what you are not, just be the best of who and what you are".

As they both hugged, they heard noises of screams and vigorous running from a far distance that seemed to build up as the noise drew nearer and grew louder.

Emerging from the ant hills far away from where they stood were countless ant heads racing toward them in descending order. One of the other ants screamed, "Look! It's the monster!" Then another ant screamed, "It's the ant eater! …ruuuunnn… for your lives!" All the ants panicked and scattered around. They all ran towards a big hole ahead of them. Nkechi ran along with the ants but when she turned to look behind them she discovered the ant eater was already getting close. The ant queen who was now behind her shouted don't wait, just go with the others; go little one. I am running as fast as I can.

Almost immediately, Nkechi felt Opaku's strong grip pull her into a hole and suddenly as if in a dream, she also heard a familiar voice calling her name.

It was her brother – Okey's voice, calling her name desperately "Nkechi! Nkechi!" He had a firm grip on her shoulders, as he shook her vigorously at the same time. "Mama! I have found her! She is here. "Everybody, she is here!" Okey shouted. "Nkechi, are you alright? What happened to you?" But Nkechi's eyes were still closed as she continued to sob and mutter over and over under her breath, "I wish I was a little girl again."

Then came Nkechi's mother, running and shouting, "Ewo! Nkechi! Nkechi! Oh my Chi!" falling to her knees as she pulled Nkechi close to herself with joy and relief. "My child, Nkechi, what happened? We have all been so worried. Your father and the other men of the village have all gone deep into the forest to search for you. My dear child, what happened to you? Why are you crying? Are you hurt?"

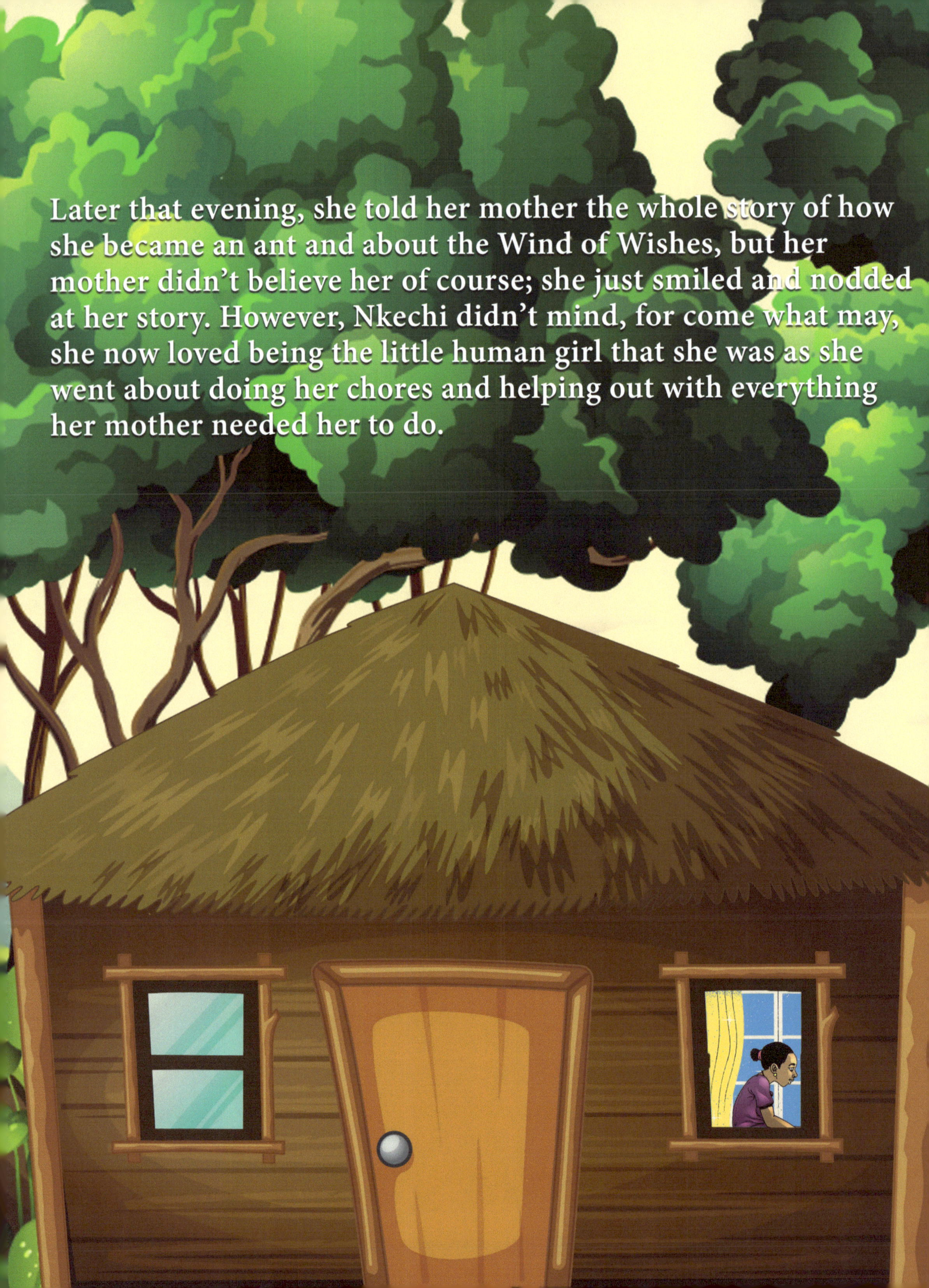

Later that evening, she told her mother the whole story of how she became an ant and about the Wind of Wishes, but her mother didn't believe her of course; she just smiled and nodded at her story. However, Nkechi didn't mind, for come what may, she now loved being the little human girl that she was as she went about doing her chores and helping out with everything her mother needed her to do.

MEANING OF AFRICAN WORDS

BIKONU- Please

EWO- (An ibo exclamation that usually expresses shock, pain etc).

5 ANT VALUES WE CAN LEARN FROM THE STORY NEEDED FOR BUILDING A GREAT NATION AS THEY BUILD THEIR COLONY.

1.SERVICE

2.HARD WORK

3.TEAMWORK

4. INTEGRITY

5. LOVE

IDENTIFY AND COLOR THE FOLLOWING
Nkech the Ant , Sweet and Banana Peel

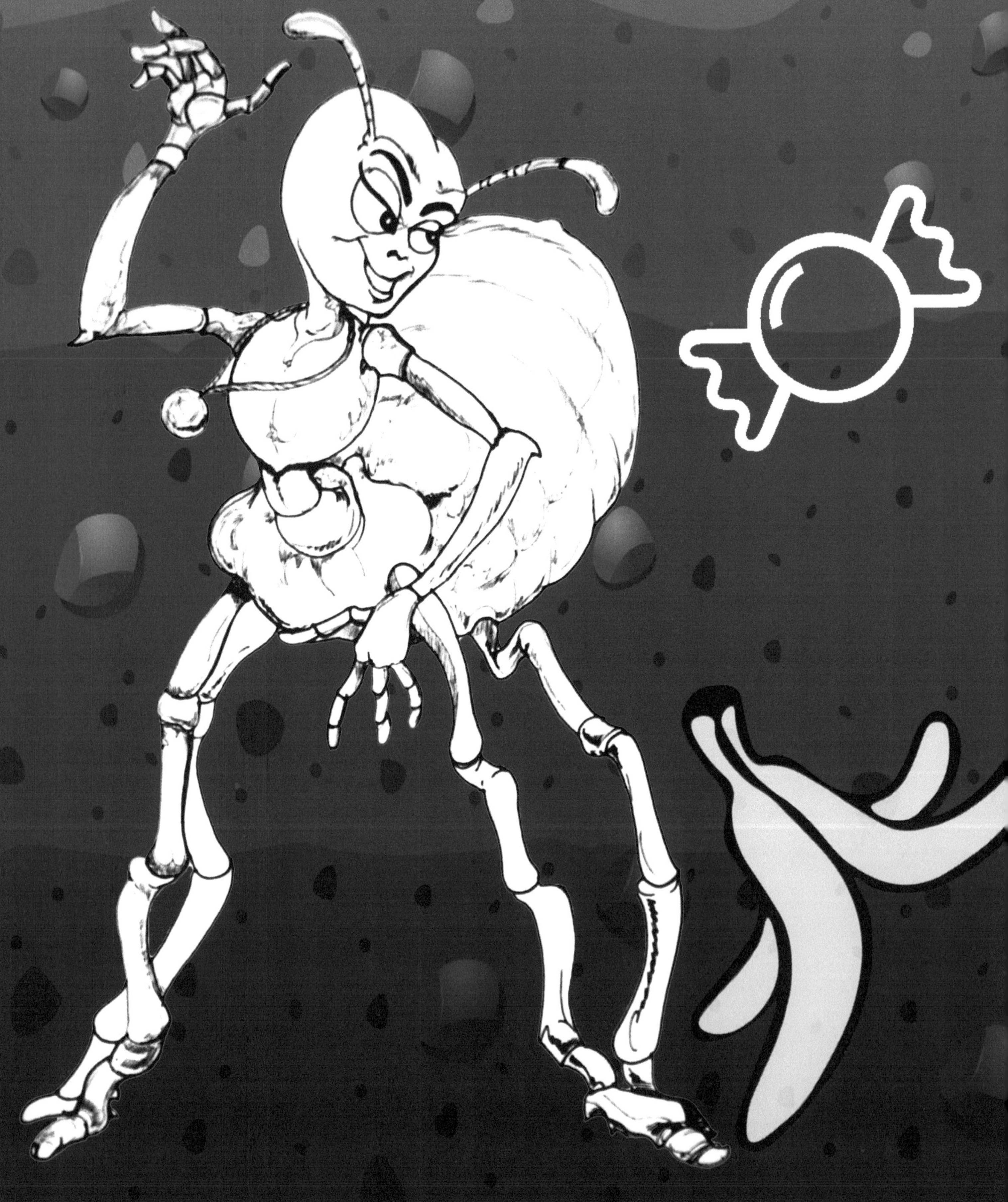